Mud Season

Justin Grimbol

ATLATL

Atlatl Press
POB 293161
Dayton, Ohio 45429
atlatlpress.com

Also by Justin Grimbol

For Heather

MUD
SEASON

A TO DO LIST

I want cheap lonely places to live. I want to loaf around. I want
to loaf hard. I want to be sweaty from doing things. I want to
kiss a person that is warm from the sun. Ideally a living person,
not a dead one. I want to cry easily. I want to earn those tears. I
want to have friends that are really old and have been divorced a
whole bunch of times.

GLOBAL WARMING

I hope the world doesn't get all dry and flaky. Or soggy like cereal. I hope Trump doesn't beat me up and put me in my locker. I hope he doesn't touch my pecker in a rough way.

COLLEGE

I went to a bar in downtown Oneonta, New York. Everyone was so young. I felt like I had stepped onto the set of *Saved By The Bell.* Living in a college town can be annoying. This is education? Are these kids majoring in short shorts wedgied up their butts?

I went to college once. But I was old. I was what they called an untraditional student. I went for four years then I dropped out. I work jobs sometimes.

MUD LAKE

The peepers at Mud Lake are really loud. Peepers are frogs that like to have sex. They like to dip. They like to get married. They like to have children.

Mud Lake was really muddy, by the way. I guess I should have known this and worn boots instead of white sneakers.

WALKING

My dog tried to kill some geese. I told her to calm the fuck down for fuck's sake. Then I heard gunshots coming from the other side of the bog. Then I found this ancient looking outhouse. I thanked God for convenient things. I put the outhouse to some use. These are action packed times we live in.

MY DOG'S TAIL

My dog wags her tail in her sleep. She also barks and whimpers. I do the same stuff. My wife will wake me up and tell me I'm okay.

"You were screaming," she'll say.

Then my dream scampers away like it had just played ring and run.

DIETING

This pizza diet is not working. And I do not care. It's too trendy for me anyway. I am moving on to a bread and water diet. Or maybe a walking-real-fast-until-the-whole-world-smells-like-a-butt diet. Or maybe I'll only eat stuff that I find in my beard. But wait. How will I get crap in my beard without eating? This is so complicated.

FIRST BASE

My dog eats poop and grass and drinks lake water and I will still let her lick my face and mouth. She is sweet and loves sunshine and running and taking long naps. My wife makes me breakfast burritos I do not deserve. She slaps me in the face with them. The small gods play Trick Or Treat and Truth Or Dare and Spin The Bible and they do this all year round and I hope one day sweatpants become hip again.

BIRTHDAY WISHES

The Schoharie creek is not far from here. I used to go there when I was little and swim in a t-shirt because I didn't want anyone to see my chubby body. It looks different now. The creek, I mean. The creek looks different because of the hurricane that came through a few years back. It moved stuff around. It fed the creek lawnmowers and some houses. It moved stuff, God damn it. Then the stuff settled, redirecting the water. And it looks different now. The long rocks my mom used to sunbathe on are under water. The waterfalls I showered under are gone too. So I have nowhere to shower ever again. Which is fine.

My wife and I live about an hour away. We drive to the creek some weekends. Then we eat at Gibby's. It's just a diner but we treat it like it's something really fancy. We order salads. Big salads. And dessert. And coffee. And soda. We never have enough cash to pay the bill and they don't take cards. So one of us has to just sit there and be lonely while the other one drives down to Stewarts and gets some cash.

A SENSE OF COMMUNITY

I just want to be part of a cult. But I only want to meet with this cult once a month. Then we can do some crazy naked stuff in the woods. Spiritual stuff. Sweaty stuff. I want to be part of a cult but I don't want to have to act happy all the time. I don't want to act blessed and enlightened and sophisticated and self-righteous. Hear me. I just want to get naked in the woods with a bunch of people and do crazy cult stuff. Maybe pass around a collection plate and collect dollar bills for my birthday.

MY DOG

The future is for skinny people only. I won't fit in.

And I don't even wear underpants anymore. I should. But I don't. I just don't. I'm going to kiss my dog's forehead until I feel decent again.

Update. I just played fetch with my dog using a one-dollar bill instead of a ball.

This also happens. I sit on my couch and try to be a writer by writing stuff on my computer. Then my dog jumps on the couch and tries to nibble on my nose. Then she licks my ear. And I laugh and tell her that I love her. This happens. This happens a lot. Thank God.

APRIL 7th

This is a moist birthday. I'm a moist birthday boy. Egg sandwiches and stuff in bed. Nobody sent me dollars. Guess I'm just going to have to pay for stuff with Monopoly money. Also, it's raining. Most of the snow is gone.

END OF THE COLD FRONT

The snow melted, making the trails around Bowman Lake soupy. But my wife felt determined to continue our hike. So we walked slowly and carefully. We hopped from rock to rock. We balanced on branches that had fallen. At times we thought we saw dry ground, but that was only a mirage. None of this was enjoyable. Even our dog was annoyed by the cold wet ground. But we marched on. And as we walked we gossiped and missed old friends and felt sappy (and soupy) about our pasts. This kind of homesickness made us long for adventure. We talked about moving out west, to a place like Montana or something like that. And we worried about our dog. What if she ran into a grizzly bear out there? Or a wolf? Or what if we ran into a crazed gun-collecting cannibal with a bear skin condom on and a fetish for chubby liberals. The world seemed scary but we had to plan these adventures because it was the only way we knew how to pray to the thing. It's how we give this life the soupiest amen we can manage.

GROCERIES

My wife calls and tells me she needs help carrying the groceries up to our apartment. I tell her I can't help her because I'm in the middle of walking the dog, even though I am actually just hiding in the bathroom holding my pit bull's powerful snout shut so she won't bark or whimper. I'm young at heart. And being young at heart means avoiding things. But, alas, growing old is inevitable. I don't really enjoy Adam Sandler movies anymore. Or at least as much as I used to. And this rock hard veiny and pulsating fact upsets me and makes me want to cry in the shower.

DOG FRIENDS

We see other dogs in the park. Usually on a leash. I ask the owners if their dogs are nice, hoping maybe their dog and my dog could chase each other and have fun. The dog walker usually looks at me like I have dropped my pants and am shaking my junksticals at them. Like I have shown them my everything. Like I have invited them to touch the thing. But I just want dogs to chase dogs. That's all.

I live in Upstate New York and people are not friendly here. When I was young, I thought being unfriendly was endearing. But now I just really hate the whimpering sound my dog makes when she wants to play with other dogs.

There are lots of pine trees at this park though. And a creek rambles and tries to cover up the traffic noise. My dog and I walk and she tries to murder some squirrels. Luckily, the squirrels don't have owners.

PICNICS

I picnicked today. I picnicked with my dog cause we love each other. This is how it happened. I was hungover and needed exercise so I hiked the trails near my apartment. First, I hiked the red trail then the yellow, which connected me to the blue. Then there was the . . . black trail. I had never been on the black trail. For a while there were signs warning about hunting season. So I feared that trail. If I walked on the black trail, hunters would pop out of the bushes and shoot my dog with machine guns. But now, with hunting season over, I decided to explore.

The black trail went on and on and on. At one point I stopped and noticed that I couldn't hear anything but a woodpecker and my dog breathing. We kept walking. Eventually we found two more trails. The neon green trail and the egg shell white trail. The forest became dense and filled with moss. The shade from pine trees looked as sweet as the plumber crack on my female friend and made me want to walk for miles. As it began to get dark, we decided to stop and take a rest. There was a steep hill. I sat on the edge of it. My dog leaned against me. Below us were a creek and a series of waterfalls. I ate a Nutri-Grain Bar and drank some water and didn't feel like a fat ass at all. Like not even a little bit.

BUMBLEBEES

The frat boys down the street have moved their furniture outside in order to maximize springtime leisure. I admire these studs. But I also hope I never have to have a conversation with any of them. That would be awful. That would be tedious and the effects would be long lasting.

I will instead spend my spring day in my back yard, getting sun burnt, drinking diet soda, reading a Fletch novel and watching bumblebees dry hump the purple flowers that are starting to blossom.

MARRIED AGAIN

Here is some information about my wife. She pets bumblebees.
And she hugs waterfalls. Her laughter smells like a dog's forehead. And our dog's forehead smells like the sun. It might even
be what invented the sun.

MORE PICNICS

We wandered around the woods and got muddy and toasty from the sun and did things, marital things, naked poking things, and we followed picnic smells until we found a park filled with families and millennials and children who didn't have a generation name yet and the picnic tables covered in carvings telling me about how JT hearted KL in 96, and there was a great view of miles and miles of farmland and more woods and towns with churches and old basketball hoops nailed to even older barns and garages and maybe down the street there is a motel with a soda machine, the old kind of soda machine, the kind our founding fathers used.

MORE CELEBRATIONS

It's still my birthday, as a far as I'm concerned. It's also still Co-
lumbus Day and not to mention it's still Mothers' Day. It's also
dead mom season. It's also spring. I thought I saw snowflakes in
the clear blue sky. Or maybe just pollen or flower petals or grass
clippings or something allergy ridden like that. Teenagers seem to
own Wilbur Park now and they heckle me and yell "hey you,
guy with the weird beard and the gray sweatpants, watch this!"
then they make really loud animal sounds, like rabid goats or
something. They know what day it is.

MORE BUMBLEBEES

Have I told you our back yard is covered in bees? Well, don't worry so much. The bees are too busy collecting pollen or whatever. They don't hover around my face with their stinky butts haunting me like a switchblade or a number two pencil about to treat my face like a multiple choice question.

And my neighbor yells at her kids a lot. The kids don't seem to notice though.

Then there are my other neighbors. They have a tree house in their yard with a large black wood-burning stove in it and I'm pretty sure that's a fire hazard.

Then there are the college kids who don't live on my block. They live in other places. But if you listen you can hear them in the distance, mumbling and yelling at the same time. You can hear them being rock hard bros. Red cups in hand. Couches in the yard. Working on their buzz. I think they are telling their parents to fuck off a little bit. Amen.

FIERCE WOMEN

I went to kiss my dog on her doggy lips and she burped in my face and it was gross and I remembered back when I was thinner, but not really thin, and just starting a lifetime of sexcapades, and I had slept with a girl in my parents' basement next to the boiler room, which I thought was haunted, and in the middle of doing it in normal positions, for like the third time in a row, I burped in that girl's face because I was so weeded and over-stimulated and worn out and young. The girl got mad and punched me in the face.

I'm a grown up adult now but I still have tiny fists, and I'm still not as tough as the girls I dated when I was young. So I did not punch my silky pit bull lab mix, I just went into the back yard and hung out with the bumblebees and enjoyed the sun. While I worked on my manly grown up tan, my neighbors' kids got in their car and honked the horn.

"Cut it out!" their mom yelled. They honked the horn some more. "I SAID CUT IT OUT!" the mom yelled. They honked the horn again. "CUT IT OUT!" and they went on and on like this for a while.

STEPHEN KING'S FAMILY

Joe Hill looks even more like his father than his father. Which makes me want to read his books. It also makes me want to smoke weed and wander around antique stores looking for Charlie Brown paraphernalia. Or throw a pizza party. Or get a hazelnut coffee from Dunkin' Donuts.

My dad drives to the same Dunkin' Donuts every day. They recognize his voice at the drive through. "You want a large coffee with that, Bill?" He gives them a big tip, then he dumps the coffee down the side of his car, and he drives backroads looking for flowers to take pictures of. Sometimes he will pull up people's driveways, just to take a picture of their gardens. These garden owners give him nasty looks but he just waves and thanks them as if they know each other. Like they went to school together a long time ago. Maybe they bullied each other. Maybe they cheated off each other during a test.

EVEN MORER BUMBLEBEES

There are dandelions out there now and the bees are having the time of their lives.

I can't tell if this is something I should be worrying about or not. I kinda love the bees. I started naming them. But Buzz looks just like Fuzzy and Fuzzy looks just like Stingy McMurtry. It gets very confusing. Too confusing. I can't handle it.

I remember one night when I was in college, my buddy took a bunch of mushrooms and booze and he had trouble standing up. He sat on the floor for an hour or so laughing and acting charming and goofy. As he sat there, a bee landed on him. I worried that he was going to freak out.

Be he just looked down at the bee and smiled.

"Look at him," my buddy said. "He's my little bee friend. We love each other so much. Hey bee friend. Can we hang out forever? You are such a good friend to me always."

It was a truly touching moment.

It was also inspiring.

That was a history in bee science.

PUDDLES

I thought it was a puddle at first but it had tadpoles in it, so it was way more than just a puddle. I wanted to get a better look. My left leg sank into the mud. It was really stuck. I couldn't move it. Cold water filled my white New Balance sneakers. I asked my wife for help. She told me to stop whining. We started arguing. We covered many topics. We fought about love and marriage and politics and movies and low carb diets and college and debt and credit cards and millennials. Was I a millennial? Or was I Gen X? I wanted to be old. I wanted to be senile. She wanted to be young and drink beer like it was tea and complain about work. My foot was still stuck and it was sinking slowly. The tadpoles were everywhere. This was a really muddy pond thing in the middle of the woods. Damn it, I just wanted to hike. We kept arguing about all the important topics. She didn't think Fletch was funny. How could that be? She didn't like Chevy Chase in general. I started to cry. We battled some more. So many subjects. We needed to be on Weight Watchers. How many Weight Watchers activity points would I get for getting my leg stuck in the mud? Not enough. More fighting. I wanted to drive around aimlessly and have adventures. She wanted a destination. I wanted to eat at crusty diners. She wanted to eat at fancy cafés run by healthy young people. I wanted to watch old movies. She wanted to watch new movies. She thought I could get my foot out of the mud on my own. I said I needed help. I begged her. She shook her head, took out her phone and turned on her NPR app. *This American Life* turned on. I love that crap. But I was stuck. I was stuck in the mud. I needed help. This episode of *This American Life* was about napping and its cultural implications. I begged her to turn the radio off and help me. She told me I was being controlling. I told her she was the controlling one. As we argued I tried to pull my foot out of the mud. But it only sunk in further. The earth was eating me alive.

MORE PUDDLES

We went for another hike. And I got my foot stuck in that puddle again. My wife used this time to argue some more. Many subjects were covered. Why did the last three or four seasons of *Roseanne* suck so bad? What's a hashtag? Won't gun control laws just make swords popular again? Does smelling a butt count as cheating?

Eventually we became exhausted. We sat in the puddle like children in a bathtub and watched the tadpoles and tried to figure things out.

MY PARENTS

I'm the son of two overweight ministers. I was raised in church, taking naps in pews and believing in the soupiest depths of my soul that God was the most boring thing ever. I hated it. I especially hated the hymns. Nobody actually sang. They just mumbled.

My mom didn't care how her congregations sounded as they sang. She loved the hymns and she sang them loudly.

My parents fought a lot. But they also liked to laugh and watch sitcoms.

They ate together too. And they gained weight. They grew great tidal wave bodies.

Then.

When I was eighteen, my mom passed.

A year or so later, my dad married an old lady. She loved hymns just as much as my mother. She never sang as loud as my mom.

But she looked proud as she sang. Sometimes she took a friend's hand as they sat in the kitchen and they sang together.

My father and she had a couple good years. They drove around backroads and watched sitcoms and ate at diners and got fat. Then she got sick. And she couldn't get better. Her body fell apart quickly. Soon she was bedridden. She couldn't go to church. Every Sunday made her depressed. She said what she missed most was the hymns.

My father and she moved to Racine, Wisconsin, far away from her home and her church. Racine was my father's hometown. He had been longing to go back. To get back to his roots. My stepmom wanted to be supportive even though it was so far away from her own home.

She spent her days sitting in her recliner watching *Dr. Phil* or the Home Shopping Network or *General Hospital,* and she mumbled hymns under her breath.

This went on for years. Then she passed away and I saw her dead body looking as yellow as spoiled sunshine and we flew back to her home church. The chapel was packed full of family and friends. And this congregation that usually could do nothing more than mumble, sang her favorite hymn. Their voices filled this tiny church. "HERE I AM LORD, IT IS I LORD." And my mind felt the kind of clarity you can only feel when you are sobbing. That this is it. This is what it's all about. This part isn't boring at all.

DANCING NAKED

There's a strip club on Main Street in Oneonta, NY. Well, it's really just a bar with a small stage, a half-assed alter for nudity and stuff. You have to crumple up dollar bills to throw them at the feet of these naked ladies, otherwise the fans will blow them away. Sometimes the girls just sit on stage and hang out and goof around with us. Once I saw this girl up there in blue jeans and a polo shirt and she danced for three songs and she did not take off a single article of clothing. I bought many Bud Lights that night.

AGING

I don't think you are an adult until you wear adult-sized diapers.
Or until teenagers start to scare you. Adults are people born in
the 1950s, I'm pretty sure. If you enjoy watching *The Golden
Girls* then you are an adult.

MY KNIFE

I find a knife in the woods. I open it. It seems dull to me. My wife and I drive away and start arguing about a bunch of stuff. So many things to fight about. String theory. Evolution. What if the earth really is flat? I want to go on adventures and find diners and pine trees and stuff like that. She wants to go on vacations and find the same stuff. But now. Right now. She wants to know why I yell so much. Is that tone really necessary? We fight as I drive around and I'm thinking the whole time about how lame it is that they built this road so close to the lake. I don't even notice until we have finally simmered down and start loving each other again, that my finger is bleeding all over the place. I had cut it open on the knife and I bled on my Jeep's steering wheel.

JOKES

Thank heaven for jokes. I love jokes so much. They are better than prayers, really. Better than church, often. Jokes and laughter. Jesus should have turned water into jokes. Not wine.

DOMESTIC SQUABBLES

Dandelions all over the place because nobody has mowed their lawn yet, and my wife and I are fighting. Our fights are vicious. We probably say stuff that's pretty mean and probably pretty funny too. Today, we were tired and sad and wanted to picnic. We had planned on having a picnic. We felt determined to have picnics. It didn't matter how unpleasant we felt. So we brought some sandwiches to Pine Lake. And threw sticks as far as we could and our dog fetched them out. We walked through the woods and then down a dirt road that went past a barn with some horses. I could smell a mixture of flowers and manure.

WARMER WEATHER

Soon it will be summer and it will be hot and buggy. It will be nibble season for those bugs that like to nibble. Like the mosquito. They love to nibble. And that's fine. Mosquitoes remind us that we have blood.

Things will happen.

Dandelions will get mowed and the sun will stir some new smells out of my old places.

The community pool will open and I will treat it like a bathtub.

I will visit my hometown on the east end of Long Island. I will swim in the ocean. Tease the sharks with my own sexy thighs and hairy little toes.

Or I will go to the creek where I dumped my mother's ashes like she was a packet of Kool-Aid mix.

I will slip on the muddy rock and fall and my wife will laugh and I will pray to her by kissing her naked butt cheeks.

And we will argue and the small Gods will listen and their tiny hands will become sweaty and nervous and that, my friends, is how humidity gets invented. Amen.

BARBRA STREISAND

My wife sees me jamming out to Barbra and she rolls her eyes. And they are really big eyes too. Too big really. She might need to get a reduction one day. She rolls them at me. She rolls them right at me and she laughs and she drools a little. She tries to suck the drool back into her mouth but it's impossible. It drips onto her sweater. She laughs some more. She talks about vacations we should go on. She talks about Vermont. She has always wanted to move back to Vermont, where we met. But I want stranger, more unscratchable parts of the country's body. I am still pretty sure there is a mystery state out there. A shadow state that isn't on the map. A state filled with diners, their countertops looking worn in and pock marked, like a guy that had horrible acne as a teen. Oh yes, a secret state where the roller skating rinks have fat guy only nights. A special state where there are lots of pine trees. Pine trees that huddle close to all the shops and roads and homes. I want to go to that mystery state. Or maybe if we can't find that place, we could go to Nebraska. "FUCK OFF ABOUT NEBRASKA!" she yells. My wife acts like I'm trying to torture her. And she's wrong. I'm trying to torture us both. Because that's the secret ingredient. You gotta have the soggiest homesickness to make your heart know how to eventually grow old together and die and stuff.

THERAPY

Andrew Dice Clay is my Carl Jung. I like dialogue and stuff. My wife is really good at being funny. We don't have roots but have other stuff. Like the shade of pine trees.

GILBERT LAKE STATE PARK

Saw an owl hanging out on the street sign in Gilbert Lake State Park. This place is a pretty ghostly park most of the year. I wondered when the beach would open up and get filled with rock hard bodies, and old men fishing, and families arguing, and sand castle contests, and, man oh man, that snack shop with the soft pretzels. I waved to the owl and give him a thumbs up to tell him he's doing a good job, a good lonely job. Nobody needs to know how many licks it takes to get to the center of a Tootsie Pop. Not really.

SUMMER

Summer's coming, and I want to look buff. Who wants to lift weights with me in a stuffy garage that smells like hot garbage? Who wants to spot me while we listen to metal and get sweaty, which is the body's way of creating juice for your friends? These are serious questions only my ghosts can answer. Or small Gods with small hands.

Instead, we walk to Twin Ferns Lake and my wife picks up some frog eggs and it feels kinda kinky in a really summertime way. The closer summer gets, the more this whole world feels like one big swingers' club.

Time to watch horror movies and learn how nudity is made.

Time to go to a waterslide park and piss in the wave pool.

I want to be reckless and drink caffeine at night. I want my pizza lukewarm. I want to watch baseball being played by fat slobs, NOT professionals. And not in big stadiums, but a town park. No mega churches, just the tiny maybe abandoned church, the kind surrounded by goldenrod. No prestigious colleges with proud students. I want public libraries filled with vagrants and the smell of piss. Instead of roots, I'll stay homesick and stretch marked and kissing my dog's forehead. I'll just wobble along and imagine what it's like to hang out in your living room. Keep it tidy for me. You got any board games? I drank diet soda and I feel ready for anything.

FAST FOOD

I like the crappy version of things. I like French fries that have been under a heat lamp for hours. Days even. I like strip clubs where the dancers just sit on the stage lazily and joke around with men who drink cheap beer. I like burnt coffee. Sometimes I don't want to hike some fancy mountain in the Catskills. Sometimes I just want to walk around the park where the public pool only has a couple feet of rainwater in it. I also like campy movies and hippie girls that are too stoned and dress like the world has ended and now all we have left is hills and tall grass and goldenrod. I like my body when it's so dirty that my wife has to put on a hazmat suit to do stuff to me, bumblebee stuff, wavy stuff, marriage stuff, naked to the max stuff. I like the way dirty armpits smell. That is easily my favorite smell ever. I like books with lots of dialogue. I like a nice too long Stephen King made-for-TV miniseries, a really cheesy one that feels like a Hallmark movie and a horror movie decided to go steady and hold hands, sweaty little hands, for an awkwardly long period of time. I like talking too much. I like gossip. I like raspy voices. I like bad jokes and bad advice and bad behavior. I miss sneaking around to smoke cigarettes. I miss how my mom had our dogs sleeping on her massive belly and how they would bark when they heard me creeping out of the house late at night. I miss how she made me huge pots of Kraft mac and cheese when I was sad and accidentally taught me how to be fat. I miss how emotionally unstable she could be and how loving that felt. I miss how obsessed she was with the OJ Simpson trial and how she bought a small TV for the kitchen so we could watch the trial during dinner. I miss how she would make me go to work with her, how I would roam the church and her office and get really good at playing with paperclips. I miss going to AA meetings with her and OA meetings and sleeping under fold out chairs. I miss getting hot dogs from 7-11. My mother loved April because that's when the doctors cut me out of her stomach, and it's when she eventually died, then got her ashes dumped into the creek in Upstate New York. She loved Easter, which usually took place during April. But her favorite holiday was Good Friday. She loved how solemn the service could be. "Remember," she would tell me, "you canNOT have a resurrection without death and grief. Too many people want to celebrate Easter and ignore Good Friday." I miss being a couch potato with her, watching sappy movies and episodes of *Roseanne*. I might have gotten too into watching movies though. Especially post mom-death. I could spend entire days on the couch watching movies. My wife used to call me an indoor cat. Which always seemed sad to me, cause I'm allergic to cats. I'm much more of a dog person. And dogs need to run through the tall grass.

MY BEARD

There are things in my beard. I think I found my virginity in there. It was mangled and hopeless. I also found some dusty sunlight that got lost in my room a long time ago. A book on how to kill an Oreo cookie with your bare hands. A map to a state that is hidden and boring. Pine trees stand close to the diners and churches and streets. And everyone flirts with each other all the time because they are too tired and goofy not to. Where spring and fall feel like the same season.

BODY STUFF

I'm starting to get used to my double chin. I feel like that's the adult thing to do.

Sometimes I sit outside and wait for the storm to come and I feel my double chin. It's soft. You should try it out.

My dog sits in the sun. She loves being warm.

Often she will roll over, belly up, spread eagle, and wiggle around, itching her back with the short grass.

I lower my chin and make its fat all bunched up and massive looking. Then I take a selfie. Then I feel sad.

The sky darkens. It sounds like a child's making war sounds. Explosions, laser fire, death moans, laughter.

I drink a smoothie. I put lots of bananas in the fucking thing.

MOIST

I am too sweaty. My soul feels like Trump's tidal wave-shaped haircut. I gotta bathe in the public pool. Feel the leisure. Feel the burn. Maybe cannon ball off the diving board for a while. No big deal. You know how it is. A storm's coming. It will cool us off. It will fill the pool with lightning bolts.

TAKE IT EASY

I see a diner. But I can't go in. Because I would have to leave my dog in the car and it's way too hot and I would never do that to her. No, we are going to have to go to the creek or the crick or whatever it's called and eat snacks there.

Swim around. Say "hi" to the metalhead who is fishing. He has Death tattooed on his chest. Death has his scythe in hand. His tattoo of Death is looking at me like, "Dude don't you want ripped pecs? This isn't even a scythe. This is a really fucked up fishing rod and I'll catch you with it. Give you a wedgie and stuff." But I don't ever wear underwear. Death should know that.

FEET

I have tan lines on my feet from my cheap sandals and my wife's face is really red after she goes on a run. And I'm insured. So I can be reckless now. Yesterday, my wife found me face down in our backyard. I was naked.

"What's going on?" she asked.

I farted. I farted a bumblebee out of my butt.

"I've had a rough day," I said.

THE HALL OF FAME

Sometimes my wife and I drive to Glimmer Glass Lake near Cooperstown and we watch the freshwater whales. Humpback freshwater whales. Big ones. We love them. We both love them so much, but I love them the most. I love how they come up and wink at me, make me feel like, hey, maybe being fat isn't such a big deal. I still got my mojo. I can make people laugh so hard their butts jiggle. Laughter can turn into dancing or friendship or memories of hooking up with strangers.

There are Amish nearby. The Amish sell really good cheese. The kind that makes you forget you are on a diet.

My wife and I hike around Glimmer Glass Lake State Park and we see the world's oldest bridge. There are carvings all over it. JL + MT 1915. It's amazing stuff. They must be so old and maybe still hooking up. Who knows.

Then we sit by the water with our dog and we eat Amish cheese. And a whale comes out and looks at us.

"Give me some of that fucking cheese," it says. "Put it on a cracker. I fucking love cheese and crackers."

TOGETHER

It's been hot and now it's raining and everything is cooling down. For a while it was getting too hot. We would go for rides with the dog and then find these beat up little diners. And we couldn't just leave the dog in the car so we would have to dress her up in shorts and a shirt and sunglasses and a visor and a fanny pack and sneakers. The people in the diner would think she was a human being. It worked a few times. But then other times our dog would crawl up on the table and howl. And usually there would be an old drunk guy sitting there and he would cheer her on, thinking that she was day drunk as well and just being exciting.

BASEMENTS

I found this book on Amazon called *Lutheran Church Basement Women*. I loved the tittle and the cover, which was an eerie shade of green and covered in pictures of old ladies' faces. I love old lady faces. And I had been listening to a lot of *Prairie Home Companion* and Garrison Keillor and I thought maybe this book would be like that. I was also missing Wisconsin and their tall grass and how aggressively humble the people there could be. So I ordered the book and got it in the mail only a few days later. I opened it up and was surprised to find it was not a novel or a collection of short stories. It was a book of recipes. It also had lots of pictures of old church ladies cooking together. As the son of two ministers, this made me very nostalgic. It's the kind of book I would buy from an antique store though. It felt slightly perverted to order a book like this from the internet.

I skimmed over the book as I took my dog for a walk in Wilbur Park. The creek was high with rainwater and I walked in it and it helped me stay cool.

My dog sniffed grass. Then ate some grass.

As I walked I saw blue jays. And I saw teenagers smoking weed.

Dark big-butted clouds filled the sky.

And I thought about that time, over ten years ago, when my wife and I went on a long road trip and we stopped at a flea market near a church in Iowa and she was wearing a belly shirt and these slightly see-through pants that kinda looked like parachute pants, the kind MC Hammer would wear. And everyone gave us dirty looks. One old lady said, very loudly, "She doesn't leave much to the imagination, does she."

ROCKS

My wife and I were swimming at this creek and the water was cold and the minnows were nibbling at me in a way that felt very intimate.

A family was hanging out down the way. They had set up towels and lawn chairs under an old rusted bridge and they looked comfortable. The dad kept throwing rocks at his son who was in the water. "Stop!" the kid kept yelling. "That one almost hit me." And the dad would laugh and laugh.

My wife and I tried not to stare.

"What do you want to eat for dinner?" my wife asked as we swam around.

"Shit, I don't know. I'm way too stoned to make a decision like that."

"You smoked weed?"

I thought for a moment.

"No," I said. "I didn't."

"So you are not stoned?"

"I guess not."

That night we had sex for a very short amount of time.

PUBLIC POOLS

Okay, I gotta go jump off the diving board with my hat still on, get all the lifeguards laughing, then, if possible, find a glob of ear wax (the Jell-o of the soul) coming out of my ear, pick it out and let it sink to the depths of the public pool with all the Band-Aids.

Dear dead ones. Help me do these things. Help me cause I'm feeling unseasonably mopey. Also, while you are at it, help me win the lottery, and get a bunch of books published, and avoid all legitimate work, and lose a bunch of weight.

Thanks a bunch. As my grandma used to say as I danced naked on the couch: I love you a bushel and peck and a hug around the neck.

HANGOVER CURE

How do you cure hangovers? Well that's a very complicated question I have some simple answers to. FIRST . . . eat a dangerous amount of Tylenol PM and eat some vitamins and then wake up and eat more vitamins and some ibuprofen. Maybe some menudo. Maybe a bagel from the Bagel Buoy in Sag Harbor, NY. Maybe just a little coffee. Just a little. Maybe some anal. Then some carnival rides. Whatever you do . . . don't shower. And don't brush your teeth. If you can, actually unbrush your teeth. Get a can of Pepsi. Pour it out. Fill the can with Coca-Cola. Post something political on Facebook. Then don't log back on for the rest of the day. Then, just before calling someone you love, check your Facebook and have an anxiety attack. Then go to an open mic. But not to read your own stuff. Just go to watch other people read out loud. Most likely you will be the only person there doing that. Then . . . Wait, what kind of hangover are we talking about? The kind you get from drinking and drugging? Or are we talking about the kind you get when you get into a fight with your wife and she turns into Donald Trump? Or are we talking about the kind of hangover you get when you have a dream about getting kidnapped, then forced to eat a gerbil, then you shit the gerbil out, then eat the shit covered gerbil? Is that what we are talking about? Fuck it. It doesn't matter. All hangovers are all the same.

WE LOVE YOU STILL

Memories of the Salt Flats in Utah make you want to stare at nothing for a really long time.

Back home. A loved one waits for you. Waits naked, with legs spread . . . because she is cooling off a chafe on her inner thighs with a fan. Cause that happens to people sometimes. They get chafed in there. Skin turns bumpy and red and tender. And they got to air it out. So they lie in bed and let the skin beg for forgiveness.

Sweat stings my eyes and I miss smoking cigarettes and I even miss church and sitting on hard pews and how garage lights flicker. And how when I was eight or nine I had the letters OPP shaved on the side of my head without knowing what the letters stood for.

I had a teacher who used to sit on his desk like a mermaid and teach us about literature. I had a mom that taught me how to laugh. I had a dad that taught me how to drive on backroads. I had a friend who taught me how to smoke weed and put that laughter to some good use. Years pass. Keep driving. Keep the gas close to empty.

I don't really party anymore but I like feeling goofy about loneliness. And let me tell you this. The best part of being fat is getting to swim with your shirt on.

DESTINATION

I want to be an exceptionally healthy and well-hung old man who does nothing but hangs out at diners and on porches and has lots and lots of women friends who smell like armpits and gives bad advice. The worst advice. The advice I have worked so hard my whole life to give.

OUR ELDERS

The trail was steep, but we kept climbing. I was out of breath and sweat was shooting out of my butt. My wife's jogging shorts had burst into flames and she had to cover her privates with leaves like people used to do way back in the day. Back in Adam and Eve times. The dog was fine though. She ran up and down and tried to kill chipmunks.

We were hoping for an overlook. We wanted a view of more hills looking pale and blue in the distance. But when we got to the top, all we found was a camper and an elderly couple sitting around a picnic table eating hot dogs.

"Steep hill, ain't it?" the old guy said.

We nodded.

"But good for you two for getting out and getting a little exercise on this hot day," his wife said.

There was a breeze. And I could smell their campfire. I didn't want to leave. But I also didn't want to intrude. So we headed back down the hill to our minivan.

"I feel good," I said.

"Me too. Sweaty and gross. But good."

MORE ON HANGOVER CURES

Okay, I'm going to come clean. I don't actually know how to cure a hangover. All I know is this. Many years ago, I was chubby and full of life and I went to a bar with my buddy, and we became very drunk and I took my shirt off and spun it around my head. My buddy spit beer on my chest and told me I had great tits. This did not go over well. The bartender kindly asked us to leave his establishment.

We drove back to my place and I got naked and I told my friend that if he really cared about me he would play with my balls. He nodded in agreement, then reached into a cupboard and pulled out a spoon. He placed the spoon under my balls and jiggled them a little. We laughed.

Then I smoked a bunch of cigarettes outside where it was nice and cool. Then we went to bed. In the morning I was not as hungover as I thought I would be and my buddy and I got breakfast at the Bagel Buoy. And we sat by the docks in town and ate our breakfast sandwiches and we fed our scraps to seagulls. There was a child playing nearby. "I could grab that child," my buddy said. "I could just grab him and toss him into the water. I could do that. But I shouldn't."

GUM ON EVERYTHING

We have a quarter and I use it on a gumball machine. Those machines are pretty hard on the soul. Sometimes you get a red gumball. And that's a great thing. But most of the time you get a yellow or a green. It's really hurtful. This night is old. I get a pink gumball. Pretty good. Not great, but pretty good. I chew it. Enjoy it. I work it over until the flavor's gone. Which doesn't take much time.

We pass fields of goldenrod. There are barns that look worn out. There are cows and stuff. There is ground that has been stomped on. There are ice cream stands and parents whose souls have been deep fried and soiled by vacation.

MALLS

There is a mall. And the parking lot is packed with cars. It's always packed with cars. But there aren't many people in the mall. Who owns those cars? I get overwhelmed thinking about it. So I totally go to Applebee's. The waitress and I chat some. I tell her I really like diet soda. The waitress tells me I'm beautiful. She winks at me. I wink at her. Then she winks at me again. Then I wink at her. She winks. Then she waits on this guy with a gray mustache. Then she turns back to me. I wink at her. She winks at me. I wink back. She winks. Then I order some boneless chicken wings. "Make them hot," I say. "How hot?" she asks. "So fucking hot." I wait and check Facebook on my phone. The food comes out. It's not that hot. It doesn't taste very good. I text my wife a cute picture of a pit bull I found on the internet. I try to get the waitress' attention. But she is fighting with her manager. Now she is kissing her manager. As they kiss one of them farts. It doesn't leave much of a smell. I think about my wife. She is really good at laughing. I need that. I need that around. Now the waitress and the manager are fighting again. Maybe he's not the manager. I notice he's not wearing pants. He has never worn pants, ever. In that case, he is probably not the manager but some guy who this waitress loves with all her heart.

THERAPY

I was late for therapy. So I had to run. I don't run often. Half-way there I got a cramp. I kept going though. I persevered. As I ran, I cursed and whimpered and prayed and made vomiting sounds and crying sounds and a sound like a pod person when he sees a stray human, I mean I started screeching like a fire alarm giving birth in a kiddie pool. People gave me worried looks. But nobody offered a ride. I got to therapy five minutes late and I ended up spending the whole hour complaining about how bad my calves hurt. He told me I should try stretching maybe. I told him I thought stretching was overrated. Then we scheduled an appointment for the following week.

WATERFALLS

We drive an hour to Burtonsville and we walk to the creek. We get in and I convince my wife to walk up to the waterfalls with me. They are short and tough and swollen and loud. She gets nervous. She tells me she just wants to hang out and swim around a little. I tell her the truth. These are humid times we live in. This water is murky but cool. My grandpa died here young and was picked at by crawfish. My mom taught me how to swim where he died. Then she taught my dad how to swim the next day. So now we act brave here. It's what we do. We float down rapids. We slip on muddy rocks. We climb things. We argue. We climb back up these strong currents. The falls are even stronger than they look. They are small but powerful. We walk up to them. We walk directly against the current. We find balance. We get close. We let the water break around us. We inch even closer. We use all our strength. We almost make it to the falls. Then we are pushed away.

MY WIFE DOESN'T WANT ME TO SHOW YOU THIS POEM

My wife came into my office. She had a creamy white streak of Nair on her upper lip. When I saw her, I started to laugh.

"How long have we been together?" she asked. "And every time you see me do this it has to be some big drama?"

I kept laughing.

"I'm going to write a poem about this," I told her. "What's that stuff on your lip called? Nair?"

"It's called 'fuck you,'" she said.

WILD LIFE

I saw this baby deer in the Wilbur Park near the public pool. People had gathered around it to watch it eat. It didn't know to run away. Nobody was going to hurt it. Still. It should have run away.

That night my wife and I tried to get a burrito for dinner. But the line was too long. The college kids were back.

"I think I hate young people," I said.

"All of them?" my wife asked.

"Maybe."

For some unknowable reason we were determined to eat at a crappy restaurant. So we went to Applebee's and ordered a bunch of apps. Down the bar was an old man with mist-colored hair. He had a tablet in front of him and he was watching a movie with the volume up high. We could hear it over the music playing on the restaurant's speakers.

"What if he was watching porn?" my wife asked.

"That would be beautiful," I said. "That would be a beautiful thing."

Then we heard a flamboyant waiter yelling, "OF COURSE I CAN BRING YOU ANOTHER STEAK! THIS IS APPLE-BEE'S FOR CHRIST'S SAKE!" He was so enthusiastic. We couldn't tell if he had lost his mind or was just really good at his job.

SHOWERS

The plumber came and fixed our shower. He told me it was fine. Our shower would survive. But I should avoid using it for a couple days.

But I'm really swampy and gross right now.

Luckily, the public pool is still open.

SPICE

I had spicy Thai food for lunch. Now I'm experiencing spicy aftermath. It hurts to sit. It hurts even worse when I take a dump. I want to scream and cry. It hurts so good. Might need an ice pack. For my butt. For the hole.

And the college kids are back and they are wearing very small clothing and that clothing seems to get smaller when they are drunk and I am way too mature for that stuff, and I cry about it every night as proof. Go away, college kids. Go. Go worship my old man beard. Worship my deep nostalgia. Go into the attic. Cut open your palm. Bleed onto the floor. See my body form in front of you. It will start as bones. Then muscle will wrap around the bone. Then my eyeballs will pop into their sockets. Skin will develop. Soon I will be a man again. Then I will have to rush to the bathroom.

THIS IS GOOD COFFEE

There's no good coffee. Not here. Not in Upstate New York. I want coffee with fleas in it. I want a coffee filled with creek water that has been cooked by the sun. I want it to be filled with goldenrod and black-eyed Susans. I don't want diner coffee in the morning. But I want coffee that tastes like a diner. Coffee helps my blood move. I want you to taste like a strip club. A special kind of strip club that feels more like a dive bar. A strip club where the stage is so impossibly far away, you have to turn your dollars into paper airplanes and you pray that these little airplanes can make it to the stage. There are many obstacles though. There are fans. So many fans. Because this place has crappy air conditioning and everyone is sweating. Put some of that in my coffee please. Do this in the morning. Do this because the crazy old people that run used bookstores in this place. Put those old people in my coffee too. Put mountains in my coffee. I want a coffee that a skunk has walked through the night before. Put my dog's wagging butt in my coffee. I want waterfalls in my coffee. I want some fat couple getting all erotic under the waterfalls please. And why are musicians always so fancy looking? Are they also models? I hate that.

GOLDENROD

The hills are covered in goldenrod. They are also covered in married people. And they are arguing. They are really going at it. Or maybe that's just my wife and I. We are the only ones arguing.

And then we stop very suddenly.

"Look at the deer bounce around in those flowers," my wife says. This is what the end of a long fight sounds like.

The college kids are back and we drive around town like we are on college kid safari. She and I met in college. We did other stuff in college too. I didn't really notice the goldenrod back then.

ELM STREET

I can never find my phone. Or my keys. Or my wallet. Or my self-respect. Or my dead ones. Or that lonely town that has a free apartment for me to stay in. Or that hard to find super secret sequel I have never seen. I have seen all the others. But not that one. That one is hard to find. It's the one where Freddy Krueger just hangs out in an old house surrounded by goldenrod. He thinks about mowing his lawn with his knife fingers. But cutting the grass would involve cutting the wildflowers and his wife used to love those so he just sits in his living room and reads Clive Cussler and enjoys sunsets and stuff like that.

MUSCULAR MOMS

I never get the creek to myself. I have to share it. Of course, I have my dead ones there. My dead mom's in there and so is my mother's father and so on. The creek is a summery Halloween soup of dead ones, as far as I'm concerned.

Yesterday, a young mother and her three little boys came to the creek. She stood in shallow water and watched her children playing in the waterfalls. They wore life jackets and they fell a lot and laughed and screamed and rolled around.

"Be careful," the mom kept saying.

She fluctuated from worried to amused to tranquil to a state of terror to relaxed again.

She was very muscular. She looked like she worked out every day that has ever existed.

At one point, she winked at me. And I winked back. She winked again. I winked even harder. Then she winked. Only this time, I noticed she had something in her eye. She was not really winking at me. Not at all.

So I rolled off the rock ledge and fell a couple feet into the water. I swam around for a while.

That night, I went to the Fonda Fair. The sun set and the sky became colorful, then dark. I walked around. I passed the Gravitron, which was called Space Invasion there. And I passed the round up and endless food stands. I wanted to eat all the cotton candy and all the greasy food but I was dieting and I managed to have some self-control.

There was a tent set up with a small church full of people listening to a young preacher deliver his sermon.

Then there was a pig race.

Eventually, I found the haunted house. It looked old. And it was covered in paintings of zombies and demons and demented wizards and a sexy nurse with bloody claws. A series of carts stood outside the haunted house. They were filled with teenagers and families. A loud siren blared for a moment. And the carts rumbled into the haunted house. I heard people screaming. Then I heard them laughing.

OLD FRIENDS KEEP GETTING OLDER

Lisa snuck away from the party with her arms full of vodka bottles. I saw her go to her tent. What was she up to? I thought.

I imagined she had friendships in there. They would be taking shots and having the best time ever. I felt left out. So I found all our other friends. I told them Lisa had snuck off.

"She's partying without us!" I said.

"That's so fucked up!" a girl named Katie said.

"I know. My feelings are hurt," I said.

"Mine too."

We snuck up to her tent, using our tippy toes to advance on her tent without being detected. Some of our other friends followed.

"SHHHHHHHHH!" Katie said.

She put her ear up to the tent.

"I don't hear anything."

"They know we are here," I said.

"How?"

"They can hear us."

"But we are whispering."

"Good point."

"But we are whispering really loudly," Katie said.

"Shhhh!"

"Wait, who'd you say was in there?" she asked.

"I don't know," I said. "It's a mystery."

"But we are all here. Everyone's here with us."

I looked around and it was true. Everyone was standing around the tent, in the darkness, not wanting to be left out.

"Everyone is here," I said.

"So then who would be in the tent partying?"

"There's people in there!" I whispered loudly. "I just know it."

Katie unzipped the entrance to the tent.

"Who's in there?" I said.

"Just Lisa."

"What's she doing?"

"She's sleeping."

"Really?"

"Yes."

"But wait," a voice came from the dark woods. "What if she's just pretending to sleep?"

"Oh that would be so fucked up," I said.

"No," Katie said. "I think she's really sleeping."

"Is it that late?" someone asked.

"I don't know."

"It's late for adults."

"But we are all adults."

"That's true."

"That is so fucked up."

"I'm going to win the party," I said.

"I'm going to win the party too," Katie said.

"Let's all win the party."

"Shhh," someone in the woods said. "She's sleeping."

"Right," Katie said. "Sorry."

"Let's go party over there," I said.

"But there is a fire over there," someone said.

"But we made that fire," Katie said.

"Good point."

MORE OLD FRIENDS

"Man jizz feels so warm at first," Katie said.

And we all nodded. We were sitting around a picnic table, drinking, and celebrating a marriage and also how we all went to college once and partied near rivers and now we all looked like grownups and none of us knew if we would be able to party like back in the day or go to bed at nine or ten or some ridiculous time like that.

"But then it gets cold," Katie continued. "And you realize all the semen are dead and you are like, AH GET IT OFF ME!"

We all nodded in deep agreement.

"That is what it is like," I said. "That is science."

HELP ME BE BALD

The college kids are celebrating Labor Day and they are being really loud about it. Most of them are majoring in partying and hijinks. This is actually just them doing their homework.

Also. There are purple loosestrife out there surrounding broken down cars and standing on the sides of creeks that have dried up.

My wife tells me it is an invasive species. It wants to party. It wants to go to school for partying then, after college, not party anymore. Maybe get a job as a party planner.

It's the circle of life.

BROS

Too many years ago my buddy Jimmy opened the bottom drawer of my dresser and found some special stuff. Stuff no bros had ever found before.

"What's this, bro?" he asked. "Is this your secret stash?"

I nodded shamefully.

He reached into the drawer. Instead of porn mags there was a stack of *Star Trek* comics. One showed Captain Pike (not Kirk) fighting a Klingon.

Jimmy laughed and gave me a very sincere hug. One of the most sincere hugs I had ever had at that time.

Then we went to the garage, which was hot and smelled like garbage, and we listened to metal and got topless and lifted weights on a wobbly bench we had bought at a yard sale.

"Look at Grimboli!" Jimmy said. "He's getting swol."

Which was short for swollen. Which was slang for muscles. I loved having muscles.

After working out we would cook steaks on the grill in my driveway.

"This is fuel," he said. "It helps us."

Sometimes friends would come over and we would get them swol too.

Sometimes we went to the beach and listened to the ocean.

Sometimes we took extremely long naps.

Sometimes we enjoyed mischief. Like this one time we stayed up all night until the sun rose and we went to the beach and we found this house that looked abandoned, so we climbed the fence. We wanted to go inside to holler and laugh and break already broken stuff. But then we noticed the house did not look old at all. It actually looked really new. Really modern even. The lights were just off. We still wanted to go in though. Then we saw lights turn on. We heard footsteps. We screamed and ran away. We jumped into my minivan and tried to drive away but it got stuck in the sand. An older couple stood on the house's back deck staring at us.

"Sorry," I told them. "We've just had a long night."

I looked at Jimmy, who was driving.

"That was a close call," I said.

"Grimboli, we are still stuck," he said.

"Good point," I said. "But I'm sure we will get out eventually."

"I hope so," he said.

SUMMERS NEED TO END

I walk through the trails near Wilbur Park and get swampy both physically and emotionally. Which is fine. Summers need to end so I can feel spooky and wear sweatshirts.

Today is too hot. It's eighty-five degrees and buggy and there is no breeze.

The trail ends at the high school. I cut across the football field with my dog. I'm a swamp thing. Plants are growing off my body. Goldenrod in my panties. Lilies in my armpits and stuff.

An elderly couple rides by me on bikes. The bikes have huge tires. They have been off-roading. Their outfits are tight and neon. Their helmets are aerodynamic.

"Cute puppy," one of the old people says.

"It's not a puppy," I say. "It's fucking four years old."

They continue riding away and I moon them with my sweaty butt. But they don't see anything because they are riding so fast.

And I get nervous. I don't want teenagers to see my weird sweaty grown man butt. That would be inappropriate.

MORE JOKES

I love jokes so much. I love to laugh. If I can't laugh, show me something sappy. I cry easily. Always have. But if I am too worn out from crying then give me something scary. Or show me a scary movie that is so bad it makes me laugh. That's a good compromise. (I feel like I have written this poem before. This is eerie.)

PORTION CONTROL

I give my dog a portion of everything I eat. I can't help it. She has these eyes. All dogs do. They are so dark, so warm.

If I had five dogs I would have to give away so much food. I would lose so much weight. I would have a body like a super-model.

If I had ten dogs I would probably starve to death. Or end up having to eat one of my dogs.

PLAN 9

And for Halloween I will be a ghost. I'll just put a sheet over my massive body. I will not cut out eyeholes. And the sheet will have a floral design. Or flannel. A grunge rock ghost. With no eyes.

I will give out the most boring candy. Do they still make candy cigarettes? If not, I will just hand out real cigarettes.

I'm restless for sure. All this waiting is a horrible thing. I might have to go trick-or-treating later today. Even though summer is just ending and it is so hot outside. It doesn't matter. I will sweat under that costume. I will leave puddles of sweat behind me. These puddles will become rivers. I will lose weight. Then, I will find it again. It's the circle of (insert fart noise here).

Sometimes my wife and I Freddy Krueger each other. That means we make love in our sleep. I will wake up and find us doing it in some strange position. We Freddy Krueger each other so often. It feels really good. It feels loving. It also feels like we are strangers or old friends or ghosts or a combination of all these things.

All I'm saying is I hope our next apartment has a chandelier.

And too many guest rooms.

MEDICINE

I had bug bites all over my legs and they were really itchy and one night I woke up with my body all contorted and pretzel-like. I was chewing on the bites. It was not working. Scratching only made it worse. I needed something stronger. I needed modern medicine. So I stumbled into the bathroom and found some stuff. In the morning my wife found a tube of cream next to our bed.

"What's this?" she asked. "Did you use this last night?"

"My legs got itchy," I told her.

"But this cream is for my vagina," she said.

"Woops," I said.

"Did it work?" she asked.

"Not really."

"Well, I'm sure it didn't hurt you."

"I hate bug bites. I need to fight back. Somehow. Some way."

I thought about things. Important things.

I looked at my wife with all the love I could muster.

"I'm going to start wearing pants," I told her.

CAMPING AT GILBERT LAKE STATE PARK

My first wife and I like going camping. We are bringing our blow up mattress. You are not really camping unless you have a blow up mattress. We will also invent fire. Then cook hot dogs over the fire. Stick the fuckers right in the flame. Watch them bubble and shrivel and mature in that way. Love is many Splenda packets. Most of the time. Not when camping though. Not when sleeping on an air mattress. God bless all air mattresses. This counts as exercise by the way.

TAKE IT ALL IN

My first wife put her glasses on this morning, then looked down at my naked body. "What the fuck?" she yelled. "Who the hell are you? You are not who I thought I was sleeping with."

"Me neither," I said.

She laughed.

"It's your turn to do the dishes," she said.

AIR MATTRESS MARRIAGE

The air mattress was comfortable and my wife's stinky breath felt familiar and loveable. I could see lots of stars through the mesh opening on our tent. I felt like I could fall asleep at any moment.

But then I heard an awkward noise. It sounded unearthly. I was sure it was aliens coming to anally probe us.

No such luck.

My wife told me they were just coyotes.

"That's scary," I said. "Are you scared?"

She said she was. But she was smiling.

"You're in cahoots with the coyotes, aren't you?" I said.

She laughed, then told me to get some sleep.

UPDATES

My computer took its damn time updating. Then it updated its updates. In that time, I went on three different diets. Got divorced, then remarried my ex-wife. The seasons changed from summer to fall, then back to summer again. Fall's right around the corner. Or so I've heard. I just want things to be spooky again. God bless all laptop computers. Especially this one. It is fully updated. It's spiritually enlightened even. Which usually just means it's unlearned some stuff, then relearned it. Hear me. I still believe minivans are a good idea.

REACHING FULL MATURITY

Time flies right up your ass. Adulthood is so 1995. Adulthood is so crushing. I need to find a loophole. Spooky stuff. You know. Things change. I used to read softcovers. Now I read hardcovers. Ghosts hide under the leaves, then sneak up and pull my pants down. What can I do? I can cry. I can sweat. I can jiggle my butt around until the whole world smells lonely.

FIGHTING

College kids are brawling. I can hear them. There's violence happening in the street outside my apartment. These kids are unleashing on each other like it's *West Side Story*. Or *The Jerry Springer Show*. And I want to go down there because fights are so much fun to watch and because maybe this is the fountain of youth. Maybe they will give me a wedgie. Or a bear hug. Or they will bow down to me and ask me for relationship advice. And I shall give it to them.

THE WOODS WERE BUSY

I thought the woods were going to be nice and lonely. But I was wrong. First, a bunch of studs jogged by. Shirts off. Glossy looking dudes. Muscles and stuff.

Then some teenagers walked by. A little one fist bumped me. "What up, big man? How you doing, dude?"

"I'm doing okay. I have had a rough week."

He nodded and walked on.

The wind picked up and many pear-colored leaves fell from the trees. I looked up and tried to enjoy the pretty nature stuff. Then some of it fell into my eye and I flailed on the ground in pain for a while.

Then I had an allergy attack.

Then I sneezed all over my shirt.

Then my dog ate something weird and I yelled at her.

I still love the fall though. I want to celebrate it with horror movies and cider and Benadryl.

HAUNTED EARLY

I went to the Downsville Diner for dinner. The place already had Halloween decorations up, even though it was still September, and the weather had just started to cool.

A tall plastic skeleton stood at the entrance. It laughed at me as I walked by. A tiny stuffed witch stood at the specials board, which said their one special was soup. That's it. That's all it said. Soup. What kind of soup? Probably chicken noodle. That was my guess, anyway.

I took a seat. The counter had the most decorations. Frumpy scarecrow looking dudes sat in stools next to me. They were made out of old clothes and masks filled with dead leaves. Their faces were turned toward me, making them look like they were staring at my lovely figure. Whoever ran this place decided to have two Halloween decorations take up those seats instead of paying customers. I loved that. This diner was really good at Halloween.

Then there was the waitress. She was unfriendly and looked as old as time and she looked at me like I had boogers in my beard. And maybe I did. I don't know.

"What do you need?" she asked.

"It says a cheese omelet with home fries is six bucks," I said to her.

"So?"

"So, how much does it cost if I add some veggies and maybe some sausage?"

"If YOU add some veggies?"

"What? No. I mean, if the chef adds some veggies. How much would that cost?"

"I don't know."

"I only have like eight bucks."

"That will be fine."

The omelet tasted so good because I was hungover. The night before I had traveled down to visit an old friend. It was his fortieth birthday. He put on a big party. There was drinking. There were jokes. There was laughter. At one point, some young men who were really into cross fit decided to wrestle and choke each other for fun. There was also dancing and fried chicken. At around two in the morning I noticed most of the other guests had gone home and the table with the chicken had been abandoned. I went to the chicken. I ate many pieces of it at a feverish pace. At one point I felt someone's presence. A lurker. I turned and saw a young, very attractive hipster girl. She looked scared. I made a grumbling sound. Pieces of chicken fell from my mouth.

The night continued. The birthday boy and I felt determined to win the party, so we stayed up until five talking about our hometowns and how much they had changed. He had grown up in Shelter Island and I had grown up in Sag Harbor. Both places were located on the east end of Long Island, way too close to the fangs of the Hamptons. And both places had broken our hearts by becoming too fancy. Now we both lived in Upstate New York, a place that couldn't become fancy no matter how hard it tried at times.

In the end neither of us won the party. It was a draw. We both went to bed around the same time.

Not long after we went to bed, his son woke everyone up. We spent the morning prowling around town with his son who was four and very charming. They were sweet together. They both got distracted by the same things. We'd pass a broken down car and they would both go "Oh wow!" Then head right for it. They both felt so comfortable around old rusty things. His son hit the car like it was a drum. We noticed a bee flying nearby. "Careful," my friend said to his kid. "I think there are some bees living in there. You don't want to get stung."

US MAIL

I ran into this greasy looking guy at the post office. He asked me if I could help him. He had a letter. And he wanted me to read it to him. He couldn't read it himself. He didn't tell me why. I told him I would be happy to.

"The letter might have personal stuff in it," he told me.

"That's fine," I said.

We walked outside and stood under a small elm whose leaves were just starting to change. I read the letter to the man. It was from his psychiatrist.

"Is he canceling my treatment?" the guy asked.

I nodded. Then continued reading the letter. The letter wasn't long. When I was done reading, I passed the letter back. The guy was doing a valiant job of holding his tears back.

He thanked me. Took a deep breath. Then he ran off.

I felt bad for the guy. I had therapy that afternoon and I was looking forward to it. Getting a letter like that from my therapist would be brutal.

Before going to my shrink, I walked around town for a bit. I went to Sal's Pizza and got a slice. The counter faced a wall covered in pictures of the owner and his family. They showed the owner when he was younger and had a perm. In most of the pictures, he was topless and had a soft body. I could see his nipples. I could eat pizza and stare at his nipples. It felt intimate.

I finished my slice then sat there and read for a while. Then I headed to therapy.

His office was only a few blocks away. It was across the street from Dollar General and the tanning salon.

It was a nice little office. Very clean. I sat in one of his leather chairs. Soft jazz played on the radio and the place smelled like tea.

We spent most of the session working on developing my Safe Place. He had me think of a landscape that made me feel peaceful. He said I could use it to fight off my anxiety. Whenever I was about to have an adult temper tantrum, or just got anxious I could think of my Safe Place and it would help relax me a bit.

First he had me describe the place to him. I really took my time with that. I went into extreme detail. And he wrote it all down.

When I was done, he read the details back to me. He used this soft voice. He is usually such a nasally geeky dude. I was not used to him sounding so sultry. And he still had smooth jazz playing in that background. It was a lot to take in.

And he kept telling me to relax.

"Just relax," he'd say. "Be in that spot. Smell those smells, listen to the wind in the tall grass. And relax. And just be there and relax."

And it worked. I felt very relaxed. If I got any more relaxed I was going to take my dick out.

I didn't want things to get weird, so I looked up. And smiled.

"I feel stoned or something," I said.

"Well, that's probably a good way to feel."

"I liked that. I liked describing that place. I liked hearing my own descriptions read back to me."

"You sounded like you knew the place you just described. Like you had been there before."

"Sorta. It's based on the opening credits of *Little House On The Prairie.*"

He laughed. Well, it was more of a cackle. Still, it felt kind and genuine.

We talked for a bit longer. I wanted him to read the description of my happy place to me. But I didn't know if I could handle him using that soft voice again. Besides, we were running out of time.

SWEATSHIRT SEASON

Sweatshirt season is here. And it's in full force.

I tried jumping in a pile of leaves. Only it wasn't really a pile. It was just some yellow leaves scattered on the ground. I belly flopped and hit the ground. I think I lost some weight from this. I'm pretty sure it counted as exercise. Diet soda also counts as exercise. So does laughing. And watching horror movies.

OCTOBER

Fall is full of charming ways of dying. The leaves have blond tips and look like they are in a boy band from the '90s. Or they look even better at aging and dying and falling onto the ground. They are colored like school buses, or chapped lips, or chafed legs, or stoned teenage eyes. They are the color of elderly laughter. Or those almost golden cans of caffeine free diet soda. They are the color of hidden butts. Of a dirty diner's counter tops. Of us taking a bubble bath in a swamp. They are colored like rotting teeth. Or a hippie college student dorm room covered in tapestries and armpit hairs and humping smells. This is how upside down lightning dresses for Halloween all month long. These trees strip so slowly we can barely stand it. I throw my dollars at trees anyway and cry. And I go on diets.

SWEATPANTS SEASON

Some days walking the dog feels like too much of an adventure. Sweatpants feel like formal wear. Writing an email is as complicated as filing taxes. Books are long.

The best Halloween costumes are lazy, like dead people who just aren't there anymore. I think I'm going to get with the times and just hand out yoga mats to the trick-or-treaters.

PUDDLES

Everyone at the park looked at me like I was deranged in some way. And I couldn't tell why. Then I saw a stain on my pants and the lower half of my shirt. It looks like pee or a masturbation stain.

"No!" I yelled. "It's not what you think! I was just washing the dishes! Some of the soapy water got on my pants! It's not jizz, I swear!"

They shook their heads. I did not look like the kind of man that washed dishes, ever. But I was. I was that kind of man. I washed dishes. Not well. But I tried my hardest.

A hundred-year-old woman jogged up to me. She lay on the ground surrounded by rust-colored leaves. I thought she was going to just give up and die. Then she did a bunch of one-armed push-ups. Then she got back up. Then she winked at me.

"Nice pants," she said.

"I was washing the dishes. Some of the dishwater got on me. It hasn't dried yet."

"I was washing the dishes too," she said.

She shook her hips around then gave me another wink.

I had been drinking too much cider. I needed to calm down. Not to mention the leaves were peaking and looking like rusty Jell-o ghosts. I knew what I had to do. I had to drive around until I was lost. Then find my way home and go onto my computer and research hemorrhoids on the internet.

NEW TRENDS

I wish the world could see me with my sweatpants hiked all the way up to my nipples, which some say are the doorknobs to the soul. I love sweatpants too much. Maybe this will be my Halloween costume. I love lazy costumes. One year I drew circles around my eyes. That was it. I just had circles around my eyes. Just circles. That was all.

"So what are you supposed to be?" my buddy asked me. "Just some guy wearing glasses?"

"Oh man," I said. "I have no idea what you are talking about."

INVASION OF THE BODY SNATCHERS REVIEW

I love the Body Snatcher movies. It could be a metaphor for many things. I like to imagine it's a metaphor for every single aspect of my life. Especially adulthood. Every time someone asks me what I do for a living, or some dopey millennial refers to someone as "uninformed," I feel like I am surrounded by pod people.

I FEEL THIS WAY PRETTY MUCH ALL THE TIME

My travel soul is Tug Boat Willy and relentless and I just want to find a diner in Montana, or Nebraska, or somewhere like that and call it an adventure.

TOO MANY FRESHWATER HUMPBACK WHALES

My dead mom is in the creek. She is sitting on a rowboat, carrying a harpoon, ready to kill. Her boat is surrounded by leaves that are the colors of freckles and skin tags and blushing. She is reading *The Prince of Tides*. Sometimes freshwater whales come up and play Ring and Run with her boat. She laughs. And her laugh sounds like a hymn.

INTERWEBS

I try and google pictures of myself naked. Nothing comes up. I'm a very nude person. But my search comes up with nothing but pictures of piles of leaves. Giant piles. I've heard about these leaf piles. An old lady once jumped in. She never came back out. She might still be in there.

WILDLIFE

We went looking for apartments in the wildernessy areas of Vermont. One lady was renting out a cabin deep in the woods. She told us about all the wildlife she had seen walking in her backyard.

Moose.

Foxes.

Porcupines.

Mountain lions.

"You ever see Garfield?" I asked.

She looked confused.

"Well," she said. "I haven't seen one of those yet, but that doesn't mean they are not out there."

LOUSY WEATHER

On our way home from Vermont, we stopped by one of those New York diners that has way too many kinds of cake and pie. The kind that has pictures of the food in the menu.

Someone had just gotten fired. People were yelling in the kitchen. One of the waitresses left in tears.

My wife and I had been fighting too. So we felt at home in all this.

We sat at the counter and ignored each other. We ordered our food and it came out too quickly.

I took a bite of my burger. She took a bite of hers.

The news was on a large flat screen hanging from the walls. Trump was mad. He said everything is rigged.

Also, there were storms and floods.

Also, we had our first frost the night before.

"How's your food?" my wife asked.

"It's actually pretty good," I said.

FANCY

My wife screamed. Her jewelry box had fallen in our piss-filled toilet again.

"You know what you should do?" I said.

"What?"

"Put the box somewhere else."

"Fuck off."

This was love for the moment. This was lazy Gods making us pray against our will.

EARLY SNOW

I'm better off tired.

Leaves are falling all over the place. Now the trees look like they got their pants around their ankles. They can't stumble though. No way.

And it's snowing at the top of Franklin Mountain and my Jeep has bald tires. And enough diet soda in the back to help me survive a second ice age.

And for Halloween I am going to be a pile of dirty laundry resurrected and unlovable and nostalgia worshipping and butt jiggling and filled with so much laughter it will cause global warming.

ADULTS

I keep aging. It's getting hard to eat my toenails.

CHORES

I thought doing the dishes naked would feel sexy. I was dead wrong. Now the tree outside the kitchen window is blushing. It's inventing redness. It's inventing third base. Then last base. Then slick roads and the great leaving that our souls want to nestle in-to.

POWERFUL BODIES

All this foliage has given the sky allergies. It feels nice. Especially when every pore of your body is crying. Even the pores in your butt. Nobody has bothered to rake yet. And that's a beautiful thing.

Last night a college kid stormed down my street. He was drunk and angry. He saw a garbage bag and he picked it up and tore it open and threw it. But there was no trash inside. Only leaves. The kid looked disappointed. I was the only other person on the street at the time. I thought he was going to fight me. But at night, in the darkness, I look stronger than I actually am. So I flexed my muscles. And he looked at me and walked across the street.

YOUNG PEOPLE

The ground is covered in leaves. And more fall whenever the wind picks up.

A millennial tells my wife and I to keep our dog on a leash and my wife smiles and nods and says "Gee thanks," in the snottiest tone possible. I feel proud of her.

We head into the woods.

Our dog smells something. Then it runs off.

"Where the fuck did she go?" I say.

"I'm sure she is fine," she says.

I panic.

I call my dog's name. I beg her to come back to us.

Eventually we hear her collar rattling. She's heading toward us full speed. I move out of the way. She flies by and jumps over dead trees and other stuff. Our dog is a gymnast.

I call her name again and she spins around and heads back toward me. She almost knocks me down. She keeps running until she is gone again.

BASEMENTS

I hang out in my buddy's basement and listen to old and rare heavy metal records. And I don't even like metal, but it feels peaceful down there because his basement is better than most antique stores, because it's filled with hundred-year-old bottles dug up from the earth, and hubcaps, and license plates for wallpaper. And he has old drunken doodles from his teenage years. One is a crayon drawing showing his childhood friend holding beers and snarling, then in jagged writing it says: BEER BEASTS: ALCOHOLOCAUST!!!

And the next day we wake up with surprisingly mild hangovers and we walk into town so his son can be part of the Halloween parade. His kid is dressed like a fireman. He thinks my name, Grimbol, sounds like Grandpa, so that's what he calls me. Grandpa. I stomp around and tell him the grandpas are hungry and they are going to get him and eat his eyes. He looks scared for a moment. Then he snarls back, "Grandpas don't eat children." He says, "CHILDREN EAT GRANDPAS!"

SPORTS

Look at me playing tennis with my friends. Look at me looking like fermented diet soda forever basement hearted. Really this is just me playing fetch with my dog in the park and we look reckless to young folks and old folks too.

GENESIS

These ghosts need to do their laundry more often. I am beginning to smell. It's an old smell. A smell from before anything had a nose. Because in the beginning the Gods sniffed their armpits and were like "Nice. I like this. We should do this more often."

MOUNTAINS

My father was visiting and we were going to head to Vermont and enjoy the foliage. We heard that it was going to snow. Since it was so early in the season, we assumed it would just be flurries at most. But it ended up really coming down and we got stuck on top of some mountain near a ski resort. At one point we saw a series of trucks pulled on the side of the road. These vehicles were tougher than our minivan. I started to remember all my car accidents I had somehow survived and the snow felt like a debt collector's call. So we turned around and we got a room at a crappy motel.

The beds were as hard as a church pew and the room smelled like pee. I stayed up all night checking the weather. The weather channel said it would get warmer by morning. Just some rain. But I didn't trust it.

My wife and I had been planning to move to Vermont. But I was wishing we had decided to move somewhere warm. Like Mercury.

I stayed up all night imagining our snowy deaths.

My father and my wife woke up at seven and we headed up the mountain. Heavy snow covered everything except the road and a creek that ran alongside the road for a mile or so. The woods looked deep. The branches of the pine trees were weighed down by the snow. There were some small homes up there and the light in the windows looked warm and the color of smokers' teeth.

"It looks beautiful," I said, as I gripped the ever holy oh-shit-handle that dangled above the passenger side window.

We made it over the mountain. And found a hotel that had soft beds and a pool. Neither my wife nor I brought bathing suits. So we borrowed some of my father's underpants and wore them as bathing suits. He's a big man. His bathing suits covered most of our body. The waistband reached all the way up to our nipples.

Once we settled into the hot tub, I embraced my wife.

"I hope the snow is all melted by tomorrow," I said.

This came across as a loving thing to say and she kissed my neck.

EXPERTS

I went to Walmart looking for their computer expert. I found a kid with long black hair hanging down from his chin. It was so thick. It reminded me of a bungee cord.

"This wire is broken," I said. "I need a new wire. Like this one. Please."

"It looks weird," he said.

His voice was soft. But not like a poet's. It was naturally soft.

He led me around the store. I didn't know where I was going. Maybe he was taking me somewhere we could both cry together without feeling judged.

We walked around for a while. Not talking. Or maybe he was talking and I just couldn't hear him.

Eventually he found the cord I was looking for. Sometimes things that seem impossible happen.

"This is like a miracle!" I said to the kid.

He did not seem impressed.

YES

Walmart actually sells great mozzarella sticks.

Justin Grimbol was raised in Sag Harbor, New York. He attend-
ed Green Mountain College in Poultney, Vermont, for four years
but never graduated. After dropping out, he moved around the
country, living in Racine, Wisconsin; Astoria, Oregon; Portland,
Maine; Oneonta, New York; and now Westminster West, Vermont.

Other **Atlatl Press** Books

Death Metal Epic (Book Two: Goat Song Sacrifice)
by Dean Swinford

Come Home, We Love You Still by Justin Grimbol

We Did Everything Wrong by C.V. Hunt

Squirm With Me by Andersen Prunty

Hard Bodies by Justin Grimbol

Arafat Mountain by Mike Kleine

Drinking Until Morning by Justin Grimbol

Thanks For Ruining My Life by C.V. Hunt

Death Metal Epic (Book One: The Inverted Katabasis)
by Dean Swinford

Fill the Grand Canyon and Live Forever by Andersen Prunty

Mastodon Farm by Mike Kleine

Fuckness by Andersen Prunty

Losing the Light by Brian Cartwright

They Had Goat Heads by D. Harlan Wilson

The Beard by Andersen Prunty